THE SPIDER

Hanns Heinz Ewers

HEATHEN SHORTS
THEIR STORIES. OUR WAY.

Published in the good ole United States of America
by Heathen Shorts, an imprint of
Heathen Creative
P.O. Box 588
Point Pleasant, WV 25550-0588

Heathen Shorts are available at quantity discounts.
Bear witness to the yackety-yak and tomfoolery at:

heatheneditions.com

Social? Tag us! @heatheneditions
Photo? Tag it! #heathenedition #heathenshort

Caution: This story may alter your mind.

First published in German as *"Die Spinne"* in *Die Besessenen* 1909
First English translation as "The Spider" *The International* December 1915
Heathen Short published January 6, 2026

Book and cover design by Sheridan Cleland
Set in 10.5pt Scotch Text
Titles in Secret Sticks

ISBN: 979-8-90075-006-4

HEATHEN SHORT #6
FIRST EDITION

And a will therein lieth, which dieth
not. Who knoweth the mysteries of a
will with its vigor?

Glanvill[1]

Paris, August 1908[2]

---

[1] Joseph Glanvill (1636–1680) was an English writer, philosopher, and clergyman. Some believe the epigraph above could have been sourced from his 1681 book on witchcraft *Saducismus Triumphatus*; however, that phrase has never been located in any of Glanvill's works. The true source is from the epigraph mis-attributed to Glanvill in Edgar Allan Poe's 1838 short story "Ligeia," which reads: "And the will therein lieth, which dieth not. Who knoweth the mysteries of the will, with its vigor? For God is but a great will pervading all things by nature of its intentness. Man doth not yield himself to the angels, nor unto death utterly, save only through the weakness of his feeble will." It's believed that Poe fabricated the quote and attributed it to Glanvill to give it an air of authenticity.

[2] In Ewers' 1909 collection *Die Besessenen*, this date is shown below the above epigraph to denote where and when Ewers wrote the story.

HEATHENRY
Thoughts on the Text

What a wicked little story, this!

First published in German as *"Die Spinne"* in Ewers' 1909 short story collection *Die Besessenen* (*The Possessed*), which notes on the story's epigraph page that he first conjured the tale in Paris, August 1908.

Six years later, the story received its first uncredited English translation as "The Spider" in the December 1915 edition of literary and arts journal *The International*[1] with the following introduction:

"The International has for many years published stories of an exceptionally high and unusual quality. Many of the finest modern short stories have for the first time appeared in the columns of this magazine. The following powerful, symbolic tale is from the pen of Hanns Heinz Ewers—the Edgar Allan Poe of Germany and one of the most notable authors writing in the German language. His fantastic imagination is perhaps best seen in the following story—unique, repelling, yet irresistible."

And while we're not entirely sure, because tracing this story's early publication history is frustratingly iffy at best, its next

---

[1] *The International* was a New York periodical co-founded, published, and edited from 1910 to 1918 by propagandist George Sylvester Viereck (1884–1962), noteworthy as the most influential propagandist for the German cause in America during both World Wars.

English translation appears 16 years later by Walter F. Kohn as collected and published in the 1931 "chills and thrills" anthology *Creeps by Night*, curated and edited—surprisingly!—by that maestro of hardboiled detective fiction, Dashiell Hammett.

Then, 31 years later, a second uncredited (we think) translation appeared in the 1962 Ace Books anthology *More Macabre* edited by Donald A. Wollheim.[2]

From there, the story began slipping into horror anthologies with increasing regularity from the 1970s onward, sometimes recycling Kohn's translation, sometimes maintaining the now time-honored custom of anonymous, uncredited meddling. Our edition happily aligns with that latter tradition, selected because we believe this particular rendering carries a modern snap and, dare we say, a little extra *bite*.

But wait—let's rewind: the seed of Ewers' story can be traced back to the 1857 short "The Invisible Eye"[3] by the French duo and masters of the macabre Erckmann-Chatrian,[4] wherein three guests have committed suicide in a specific room of an old inn and an artist arrives to solve the mystery. And, whether intentional or not, Ewers spun his inspiration with a delightful little loop-the-loop: "The Invisible Eye" is set in a hotel in Nuremberg, Germany, and was first written in French, whereas "The Spider" is set in a hotel in Paris, France, and was first written in German. *C'est wunderbar!*

As for the text, given this translation's modernity little ~~editing~~ Heathening was required on our part. The bulk of our work lies in the twenty-odd footnotes we've appended for context, clarity, and commentary where necessary.

Finally, we must . . . we must . . . must . . . and then . . .

---

[2] Donald Allen Wollheim (1914–1990) was an American science fiction editor, publisher, and author.

[3] The original French title was *L'oeil invisible ou L'auberge des trois pendus* ("The Invisible Eye, or The Inn of the Three Hanged Men").

[4] The name used by French authors Émile Erckmann (1822–1899) and Alexandre Chatrian (1826–1890), nearly all of whose works were jointly written.

THE SPIDER

When the student of medicine, Richard Bracquemont, decided to move into room #7 of the small Hotel Stevens, Rue Alfred Stevens (Paris 6),[1] three persons had already hanged themselves from the crossbar of the window in that room on three successive Fridays.

The first was a Swiss traveling salesman. They found his corpse on Saturday evening. The doctor determined that the death must have occurred between five and six o'clock on Friday afternoon. The corpse hung on a strong hook that had been driven into the window's crossbar to serve as a hanger for articles of clothing. The window was closed, and the dead man had used the curtain cord as a noose. Since the window was very low, he hung with his knees practically touching the floor—a sign of the great discipline the suicide must have exercised in carrying out his design. Later, it was learned that he was a married man, a father. He had been a man of a continually happy disposition; a man who had achieved a secure place in life. There was not one written word to be found that would have shed light on his suicide . . . not even a will. Furthermore, none of his acquaintances could recall hearing anything at all from him that would have permitted anyone to predict his end.

The second case was not much different. The artist, Karl

---

[1] A fictional setting invented by Ewers.

Krause, a high wire cyclist in the nearby Medrano Circus,[2] moved into room #7 two days later. When he did not show up at Friday's performance, the director sent an employee to the hotel. There, he found Krause in the unlocked room hanging from the window crossbar in circumstances exactly like those of the previous suicide. This death was as perplexing as the first. Krause was popular. He earned a very high salary, and had appeared to enjoy life at its fullest. Once again, there was no suicide note; no sinister hints. Krause's sole survivor was his mother to whom the son had regularly sent 300 marks[3] on the first of the month.

For Madame Dubonnet, the owner of the small, cheap guesthouse whose clientele was composed almost completely of employees in a nearby Montmartre vaudeville theater, this second curious death in the same room had very unpleasant consequences. Already several of her guests had moved out, and other regular clients had not come back. She appealed for help to her personal friend, the inspector of police of the ninth precinct, who assured her that he would do everything in his power to help her. He pushed zealously ahead not only with the investigation into the grounds for the suicides of the two guests, but he also placed an officer in the mysterious room. This man, Charles-Maria Chaumié, actually volunteered for the task. Chaumié was an old "Marsouin,"[4] a marine sergeant with eleven years of service, who had lain so many nights at posts in Tonkin[5] and Annam,[6] and had greeted so many stealthily creeping river pirates with a shot from his rifle that he seemed ideally suited to encounter the "ghost" that everyone on Rue Alfred Stevens was talking about.

[2] Formerly located at 63 Boulevard de Rochechouart in Paris, the Cirque Medrano is a French circus that is still active today as a successful traveling circus.

[3] A mark is the basic monetary unit of Germany.

[4] A nickname of the *Troupes de Marine* (Marine Troops) of the French Army.

[5] A mountainous region of northern Vietnam.

[6] A subdivision of French Indochina, now the central region of Vietnam.

From then on, each morning and each evening, Chaumié paid a brief visit to the police station to make his report, which, for the first few days, consisted only of his statement that he had not noticed anything unusual. On Wednesday evening, however, he hinted that he had found a clue. Pressed to say more, he asked to be allowed more time before making any comment, since he was not sure that what he had discovered had any relationship to the two deaths, and he was afraid he might say something that would make him look foolish.

On Thursday, his behavior seemed a bit uncertain, but his mood was noticeably more serious. Still, he had nothing to report. On Friday morning, he came in very excited and spoke, half humorously, half seriously, of the strangely attractive power that his window had. He would not elaborate this notion and said that, in any case, it had nothing to do with the suicides; and that it would be ridiculous of him to say any more. When, on that same Friday, he failed to make his regular evening report, someone went to his room and found him hanging from the crossbar of the window.

All the circumstances, down to the minutest detail, were the same here as in the previous cases. Chaumié's legs dragged along the ground. The curtain cord had been used for a noose. The window was closed, the door to the room had not been locked and death had occurred at six o'clock. The dead man's mouth was wide open, and his tongue protruded from it.

Chaumié's death, the third in as many weeks in room #7, had the following consequences: all the guests, with the exception of a German high-school teacher in room #16, moved out. The teacher took advantage of the occasion to have his rent reduced by a third. The next day, Mary Garden, the famous Opéra Comique[7] singer, drove up to the Hotel Stevens and paid two hundred francs for the red curtain cord, saying it would bring

---

[7] A Paris opera company founded in 1714 and officially known as *Théâtre national de l'Opéra-Comique.*

ends p. 26

her luck. The story, small consolation for Madame Dubonnet, got into the papers.

If these events had occurred in summer, in July or August, Madame Dubonnet would have secured three times that price for her cord, but as it was in the middle of a troubled year, with elections, disorders in the Balkans,[8] bank crashes in New York,[9] the visit of the King and Queen of England, the result was that the *affaire Rue Alfred Stevens* was talked of less than it deserved to be. As for the newspaper accounts, they were brief, being essentially the police reports word for word.

These reports were all that Richard Bracquemont, the medical student, knew of the matter. There was one detail about which he knew nothing because neither the police inspector nor any of the eyewitnesses had mentioned it to the press. It was only later, after what happened to the medical student, that anyone remembered that when the police removed Sergeant Charles-Maria Chaumié's body from the window crossbar a large black spider crawled from the dead man's open mouth. A hotel porter flicked it away, exclaiming, "Ugh, another of those damned creatures." When in later investigations which concerned themselves mostly with Bracquemont the servant was interrogated, he said that he had seen a similar spider crawling on the Swiss traveling salesman's shoulder when his body was removed from the window crossbar. But Richard Bracquemont knew nothing of all this.

It was more than two weeks after the last suicide that Bracquemont moved into the room. It was a Sunday. Bracquemont conscientiously recorded everything that happened to him in his journal.

That journal now follows . . .

---

[8] In 1907, the Balkans were a powder keg of nationalism and imperial competition, all leading toward the Balkan Wars and eventually World War I.

[9] The Panic of 1907 was a financial crisis that occurred when the New York Stock Exchange suddenly fell almost 50% from its peak the previous year.

Monday, February 28

I moved in yesterday evening. I unpacked my two wicker suitcases and straightened the room a little. Then I went to bed. I slept so soundly that it was nine o'clock the next morning before a knock at my door woke me. It was my hostess, bringing me breakfast herself. One could read her concern for me in the eggs, the bacon and the superb *café au lait*[10] she brought me. I washed and dressed, then smoked a pipe as I watched the servant make up the room.

So, here I am. I know well that the situation may prove dangerous, but I think I may just be the one to solve the problem. If, once upon a time, Paris was worth a mass (conquest comes at a dearer rate these days), it is well worth risking my life *pour un si bel enjeu.*[11] I have at least one chance to win, and I mean to risk it.

As it is, I'm not the only one who has had this notion. Twenty-seven people have tried for access to the room. Some went to the police, some went directly to the hotel owner. There were even three women among the candidates. There was plenty of competition. No doubt the others are poor devils like me.

And yet, it was I who was chosen. Why? Because I was the only one who hinted that I had some plan—or the semblance of a plan. Naturally, I was bluffing.

These journal entries are intended for the police. I must say that it amuses me to tell those gentlemen how neatly I fooled them. If the Inspector has any sense, he'll say, "Hm. This Bracquemont is just the man we need." In any case, it doesn't matter

---

[10] Coffee with milk.
[11] French: "for such a beautiful challenge."

ends p. 26

what he'll say. The point is I'm here now, and I take it as a good sign that I've begun my task by bamboozling the police. I had gone first to Madame Dubonnet, and it was she who sent me to the police. They put me off for a whole week—as they put off my rivals as well. Most of them gave up in disgust, having something better to do than hang around the musty squad room. The Inspector was beginning to get irritated at my tenacity. At last, he told me I was wasting my time. That the police had no use for bungling amateurs. "Ah, if only you had a plan. Then . . ."

On the spot, I announced that I had such a plan, though naturally I had no such thing. Still, I hinted that my plan was brilliant, but dangerous, that it might lead to the same end as that which had overtaken the police officer, Chaumié. Still, I promised to describe it to him if he would give me his word that he would personally put it into effect. He made excuses, claiming he was too busy but when he asked me to give him at least a hint of my plan, I saw that I had piqued his interest.

I rattled off some nonsense made up of whole cloth.[12] God alone knows where it all came from. I told him that six o'clock of a Friday is an occult hour. It is the last hour of the Jewish week; the hour when Christ disappeared from his tomb and descended into hell. That he would do well to remember that the three suicides had taken place at approximately that hour.[13]

[12] The idiom "made up of whole cloth" (also "cut from whole cloth") means something is a complete fabrication or fiction. The phrase originates from the idea of cloth woven in one continuous piece.

[13] In Jewish tradition, the week ends not at 6 PM but at sunset on Friday, when the Sabbath (*Shabbat*) begins. Some Christian liturgical traditions use 6 PM as a symbolic "fixed" sunset, which may explain Ewers' clock-time. His reference to Christ alludes to the Harrowing of Hell (*Descensus Christi ad Inferos*), the belief that after dying at the "ninth hour" (about 3 PM) on Good Friday, Jesus was buried before sunset in accordance with Jewish law and then descended to *Sheol*/Hades during the interval between death and Resurrection. While no doctrine assigns this descent specifically to 6 PM, Ewers collapses these traditions into a single liminal moment. In folklore, dusk is the "gray hour," a time of disorientation; in occult lore, such thresholds—between day and night, life and death—are moments when the veil between worlds is thinnest.

That was all I could tell him just then, I said, but I pointed him to *The Revelations of St. John.*[14]

The Inspector assumed the look of a man who understood all that I had been saying, then he asked me to come back that evening.

I returned, precisely on time, and noted a copy of the *New Testament* on the Inspector's desk. I had, in the meantime, been at the *Revelations* myself without however having understood a syllable. Perhaps the Inspector was cleverer than I. Very politely—nay—deferentially, he let me know that, despite my extremely vague intimations, he believed he grasped my line of thought and was ready to expedite my plan in every way.

And here, I must acknowledge that he has indeed been tremendously helpful. It was he who made the arrangement with the owner that I was to have anything I needed so long as I stayed in the room. The Inspector gave me a pistol and a police whistle, and he ordered the officers on the beat to pass through the Rue Alfred Stevens as often as possible, and to watch my window for any signal. Most important of all, he had a desk telephone installed which connects directly with the police station. Since the station is only four minutes away, I see no reason to be afraid.

Wednesday, March 1

Nothing has happened. Not yesterday. Not today.

Madame Dubonnet brought a new curtain cord from another room—the rooms are mostly empty, of course. Madame Dubonnet takes every opportunity to visit me, and each time she brings something with her. I have asked her to tell me again everything

---

[14] *The Revelation of St. John* (also called the *Book of Revelation,* the *Book of the Apocalypse,* or the *Apocalypse of John*) is the final book of the New Testament, a prophetic and symbolic text filled with vivid imagery of Christ's glorious return and God's ultimate victory.

ends p. 26

that happened here, but I have learned nothing new. She has her own opinion of the suicides. Her view is that the music hall artist, Krause, killed himself because of an unhappy love affair. During the last year that Krause lived in the hotel, a young woman had made frequent visits to him. These visits had stopped, just before his death. As for the Swiss gentleman, Madame Dubonnet confessed herself baffled. On the other hand, the death of the policeman was easy to explain. He had killed himself just to annoy her.

These are sad enough explanations, to be sure, but I let her babble on to take the edge off my boredom.

Thursday, March 3

Still nothing. The Inspector calls twice a day. Each time, I tell him that all is well. Apparently, these words do not reassure him.

I have taken out my medical books and I study, so that my self-imposed confinement will have some purpose.

Friday, March 4

I ate uncommonly well at noon. The landlady brought me half a bottle of champagne. It seemed a meal for a condemned man. Madame Dubonnet looked at me as if I were already three-quarters dead. As she was leaving, she begged me tearfully to come with her, fearing no doubt that I would hang myself "just to annoy her."

I studied the curtain cord once again. Would I hang myself with it? Certainly, I felt little desire to do so. The cord is stiff and rough—not the sort of cord one makes a noose of. One would need to be truly determined before one could imitate the others.

I am seated now at my table. At my left, the telephone. At my right, the revolver. I'm not frightened; but I am curious.

Six o'clock, the same evening

Nothing has happened. I was about to add, "Unfortunately." The fatal hour has come—and has gone, like any six o'clock on any evening. I won't hide the fact that I occasionally felt a certain impulse to go to the window, but for a quite different reason than one might imagine. The Inspector called me at least ten times between five and six o'clock. He was as impatient as I was. Madame Dubonnet, on the other hand, is happy. A week has passed without someone in #7 hanging himself. Marvelous.

Monday, March 7

I have a growing conviction that I will learn nothing; that the previous suicides are related to the circumstances surrounding the lives of the three men. I have asked the Inspector to investigate the cases further, convinced that someone will find their motivations. As for me, I hope to stay here as long as possible. I may not conquer Paris here, but I live very well and I'm fattening up nicely. I'm also studying hard, and I am making real progress. There is another reason, too, that keeps me here.

Wednesday, March 9

So! I have taken one step more. Clarimonda.

I haven't yet said anything about Clarimonda. It is she who is my "third" reason for staying here. She is also the reason I was tempted to go to the window during the "fateful" hour last Friday. But of course, not to hang myself.

Clarimonda. Why do I call her that? I have no idea what her name is, but it ought to be Clarimonda. When finally I ask her

ends p. 26

name, I'm sure it will turn out to be Clarimonda. I noticed her almost at once . . . in the very first days. She lives across the narrow street; and her window looks right into mine. She sits there, behind her curtains.

I ought to say that she noticed me before I saw her; and that she was obviously interested in me. And no wonder. The whole neighborhood knows I am here, and why. Madame Dubonnet has seen to that.

I am not of a particularly amorous disposition. In fact, my relations with women have been rather meager. When one comes from Verdun to Paris to study medicine, and has hardly money enough for three meals a day, one has something else to think about besides love. I am then not very experienced with women, and I may have begun my adventure with her stupidly. Never mind. It's exciting just the same.

At first, the idea of establishing some relationship with her simply did not occur to me. It was only that, since I was here to make observations, and, since there was nothing in the room to observe, I thought I might as well observe my neighbor—openly, professionally. Anyhow, one can't sit all day long just reading.

Clarimonda, I have concluded, lives alone in the small flat across the way. The flat has three windows, but she sits only before the window that looks into mine. She sits there, spinning on an old-fashioned spindle, such as my grandmother inherited from a great aunt. I had no idea anyone still used such spindles. Clarimonda's spindle is a lovely object. It appears to be made of ivory; and the thread she spins is of an exceptional fineness. She works all day behind her curtains, and stops spinning only as the sun goes down. Since darkness comes abruptly here in this narrow street and in this season of fogs, Clarimonda disappears from her place at five o'clock each evening. I have never seen a light in her flat.

What does Clarimonda look like? I'm not quite sure. Her hair is black and wavy; her face pale. Her nose is short and finely shaped with delicate nostrils that seem to quiver. Her lips, too, are pale: and when she smiles, it seems that her small teeth are as keen as those of some beast of prey. Her eyelashes are long and dark; and her huge dark eyes have an intense glow. I guess all these details more than I know them. It is hard to see clearly through the curtains.

Something else: she always wears a black dress embroidered with a lilac motif; and black gloves, no doubt to protect her hands from the effects of her work. It is a curious sight: her delicate hands moving perpetually, swiftly grasping the thread, pulling it, releasing it, taking it up again; as if one were watching the indefatigable[15] motions of an insect.

Our relationship? For the moment, still very superficial, though it *feels* deeper. It began with a sudden exchange of glances in which each of us noted the other. I must have pleased her, because one day she studied me a while longer, then smiled tentatively. Naturally, I smiled back. In this fashion, two days went by, each of us smiling more frequently with the passage of time. Yet something kept me from greeting her directly.

Until today. This afternoon, I did it. And Clarimonda returned my greeting. It was done subtly enough, to be sure, but I saw her nod.

Thursday, March 10

Yesterday, I sat for a long time over my books, though I can't truthfully say that I studied much. I built castles in the air and dreamed of Clarimonda.

I slept fitfully.

This morning, when I approached my window, Clarimonda

---

[15] Tireless; unrelenting.

ends p. 26

was already in her place. I waved, and she nodded back. She laughed and studied me for a long time.

I tried to read, but I felt much too uneasy. Instead, I sat down at my window and gazed at Clarimonda. She too had laid her work aside. Her hands were folded in her lap. I drew my curtain wider with the window cord, so that I might see better. At the same moment, Clarimonda did the same with the curtains at her window. We exchanged smiles.

We must have spent a full hour gazing at each other.

Finally, she took up her spinning.

Saturday, March 12

The days pass. I eat and drink. I sit at the desk. I light my pipe; I look down at my book but I don't read a word, though I try again and again. Then I go to the window where I wave to Clarimonda. She nods. We smile. We stare at each other for hours.

Yesterday afternoon, at six o'clock, I grew anxious. The twilight came early, bringing with it something like anguish. I sat at my desk. I waited until I was invaded by an irresistible need to go to the window—not to hang myself; but just to see Clarimonda. I sprang up and stood beside the curtain where it seemed to me I had never been able to see so clearly, though it was already dark. Clarimonda was spinning, but her eyes looked into mine. I felt myself strangely contented even as I experienced a light sensation of fear.

The telephone rang. It was the Inspector tearing me out of my trance with his idiotic questions. I was furious.

This morning, the Inspector and Madame Dubonnet visited me. She is enchanted with how things are going. I have now lived for two weeks in room #7. The Inspector, however, does not feel he is getting results. I hinted mysteriously that I was on the trail of something most unusual. The jackass took me at my word and fulfilled my dearest wish. I've been allowed to stay in the room for another week. God knows it isn't Madame Dubonnet's cooking or wine-cellar that keeps me here. How quickly one can be sated with such things. No. I want to stay because of the window Madame Dubonnet fears and hates. That beloved window that shows me Clarimonda. I have stared out of my window, trying to discover whether she ever leaves her room, but I've never seen her set foot on the street.

As for me, I have a large, comfortable armchair and a green shade over the lamp whose glow envelopes me in warmth. The Inspector has left me with a huge packet of fine tobacco—and yet I cannot work. I read two or three pages only to discover that I haven't understood a word. My eyes see the letters, but my brain refuses to make any sense of them. Absurd. As if my brain were posted: "No Trespassing." It is as if there were no room in my head for any other thought than the one: Clarimonda. I push my books away; I lean back deeply into my chair. I dream.

Sunday, March 13

This morning I watched a tiny drama while the servant was tidying my room. I was strolling in the corridor when I paused before a small window in which a large garden spider had her web. Madame Dubonnet will not have it removed because she believes spiders bring luck, and she's had enough misfortunes in her house lately. Today, I saw a much smaller spider, a male, moving across the strong threads toward the middle of the web, but when his movements alerted the female, he drew back shyly to the edge of the web from which he made a second attempt to cross it. Finally, the female in the middle appeared attentive to his wooing, and stopped moving. The male tugged at a strand gently, then more strongly till the whole web shook. The female

ends p. 26

stayed motionless. The male moved quickly forward and the female received him quietly, calmly, giving herself over completely to his embraces. For a long minute, they hung together motionless at the center of the huge web.

Then I saw the male slowly extricating himself, one leg over the other. It was as if he wanted tactfully to leave his companion alone in the dream of love, but as he started away, the female, overwhelmed by a wild life, was after him, hunting him ruthlessly. The male let himself drop from a thread; the female followed, and for a while the lovers hung there, imitating a piece of art. Then they fell to the window-sill where the male, summoning all his strength, tried again to escape. Too late. The female already had him in her powerful grip, and was carrying him back to the center of the web. There, the place that had just served as the couch for their lascivious embraces took on quite another aspect. The lover wriggled, trying to escape from the female's wild embrace, but she was too much for him. It was not long before she had wrapped him completely in her thread, and he was helpless. Then she dug her sharp pincers into his body, and sucked full draughts[16] of her young lover's blood. Finally, she detached herself from the pitiful and unrecognizable shell of his body and threw it out of her web.

So that is what love is like among these creatures. Well for me that I am not a spider.

Monday, March 14

I don't look at my books any longer. I spend my days at the window. When it is dark, Clarimonda is no longer there, but if I close my eyes, I continue to see her.

This journal has become something other than I intended. I've spoken about Madame Dubonnet, about the Inspector;

---

[16] In this context, a draught is the amount swallowed in a single act of drinking.

about spiders and about Clarimonda. But I've said nothing about the discoveries I undertook to make. It can't be helped.

Tuesday, March 15

We have invented a strange game, Clarimonda and I. We play it all day long. I greet her; then she greets me. Then I tap my fingers on the windowpanes. The moment she sees me doing that, she too begins tapping. I wave to her; she waves back. I move my lips as if speaking to her; she does the same. I run my hand through my sleep-disheveled hair and instantly her hand is at her forehead. It is a child's game, and we both laugh over it. Actually, she doesn't laugh. She only smiles a gently contained smile. And I smile back in the same way.

The game is not as trivial as it seems. It's not as if we were grossly imitating each other—that would weary us both. Rather, we are communicating with each other. Sometimes, telepathically, it would seem, since Clarimonda follows my movements instantaneously almost before she has had time to see them. I find myself inventing new movements, or new combinations of movements, but each time she repeats them with disconcerting speed. Sometimes. I change the order of the movements to surprise her, making whole series of gestures as rapidly as possible; or I leave out some motions and weave in others, the way children play "Simon Says."[17] What is amazing is that Clarimonda never once makes a mistake, no matter how quickly I change gestures.

That's how I spend my days . . . but never for a moment do

---

[17] A game in which one player assumes the role of "Simon" and issues instructions to the other players, which should be followed only when preceded by the phrase "Simon says." Players are eliminated from the game when following instructions that do not include the phrase, or by failing to follow an instruction which does include the phrase.

ends p. 26

I feel that I'm killing time. It seems, on the contrary, that never in my life have I been better occupied.

Wednesday, March 16

Isn't it strange that it hasn't occurred to me to put my relationship with Clarimonda on a more serious basis than these endless games. Last night, I thought about this . . . I can, of course, put on my hat and coat, walk down two flights of stairs, take five steps across the street and mount two flights to her door which is marked with a small sign that says "Clarimonda." Clarimonda what? I don't know. Something. Then I can knock and . . .

Up to this point I imagine everything very clearly, but I cannot see what should happen next. I know that the door opens. But then I stand before it, looking into a dark void. Clarimonda doesn't come. Nothing comes. Nothing is there, only the black, impenetrable dark.

Sometimes, it seems to me that there can be no other Clarimonda but the one I see in the window; the one who plays gesture-games with me. I cannot imagine a Clarimonda wearing a hat, or a dress other than her black dress with the lilac motif. Nor can I imagine a Clarimonda without black gloves. The very notion that I might encounter Clarimonda somewhere in the streets or in a restaurant eating, drinking, or chatting is so improbable that it makes me laugh.

Sometimes I ask myself whether I love her. It's impossible to say, since I have never loved before. However, if the feeling that I have for Clarimonda is really—love, then love is something entirely different from anything I have seen among my friends or read about in novels. It is hard for me to be sure of my feelings and harder still to think of anything that doesn't relate to Clarimonda or, what is more important, to our game. Undeniably, it is our game that concerns me. Nothing else—and this is what I understand least of all.

There is no doubt that I am drawn to Clarimonda, but with this attraction there is mingled another feeling, fear. No. That's not it either. Say rather a vague apprehension in the presence of the unknown. And this anxiety has a strangely voluptuous quality so that I am at the same time drawn to her even as I am repelled by her. It is as if I were moving in giant circles around her, sometimes coming close, sometimes retreating . . . back and forth, back and forth. Once, I am sure of it, it will happen, and I will join her.

Clarimonda sits at her window and spins her slender, eternally fine thread, making a strange cloth whose purpose I do not understand. I am amazed that she is able to keep from tangling her delicate thread. Hers is surely a remarkable design, containing mythical beasts and strange masks.

Thursday, March 17

I am curiously excited. I don't talk to people any more. I barely say "hello" to Madame Dubonnet or to the servant. I hardly give myself time to eat. All I can do is sit at the window and play the game with Clarimonda. It is an enthralling game. Overwhelming.

I have the feeling something will happen tomorrow.

Friday, March 18

Yes. Yes. Something will happen today. I tell myself—as loudly as I can—that that's why I am here. And yet, horribly enough, I am afraid. And in the fear that the same thing is going to happen to me as happened to my predecessors, there

ends p. 26

is strangely mingled another fear: a terror of Clarimonda. And I cannot separate the two fears.

I am frightened. I want to scream.

Six o'clock, evening

I have my hat and coat on. Just a couple of words.

At five o'clock, I was at the end of my strength. I'm perfectly aware now that there is a relationship between my despair and the "sixth hour" that was so significant in the previous weeks. I no longer laugh at the trick I played the Inspector.

I was sitting at the window, trying with all my might to stay in my chair, but the window kept drawing me. I had to resume the game with Clarimonda. And yet, the window horrified me. I saw the others hanging there: the Swiss traveling salesman, fat, with a thick neck and a gray stubbly beard; the thin artist; and the powerful police sergeant. I saw them, one after the other, hanging from the same hook, their mouths open, their tongues sticking out. And then, I saw myself among them.

Oh, this unspeakable fear. It was clear to me that it was provoked as much by Clarimonda as by the crossbar and the horrible hook. May she pardon me . . . but it is the truth. In my terror, I keep seeing the three men hanging there, their legs dragging on the floor.

And yet, the fact is I had not felt the slightest desire to hang myself; nor was I afraid that I would want to do so. No, it was the window I feared; and Clarimonda. I was sure that something horrid was going to happen. Then I was overwhelmed by the need to go to the window—to stand before it. I had to . . .

The telephone rang. I picked up the receiver and before I could hear a word, I screamed, "Come. Come at once."

It was as if my shrill cry had in that instant dissipated the shadows from my soul. I grew calm. I wiped the sweat from my forehead. I drank a glass of water. Then I considered what I should say to the Inspector when he arrived. Finally, I went to the window. I waved and smiled. And Clarimonda too waved and smiled.

Five minutes later, the Inspector was here. I told him that I was getting to the bottom of the matter, but I begged him not to question me just then. That very soon I would be in a position to make important revelations. Strangely enough, though I was lying to him. I myself had the feeling that I was telling the truth. Even now, against my will, I have that same conviction.

The Inspector could not help noticing my agitated state of mind, especially since I apologized for my anguished cry over the telephone. Naturally, I tried to explain it to him, and yet I could not find a single reason to give for it. He said affectionately that there was no need ever to apologize to him; that he was always at my disposal; that that was his duty. It was better that he should come a dozen times to no effect rather than fail to be here when he was needed. He invited me to go out with him for the evening. It would be a distraction for me. It would do me good not to be alone for a while. I accepted the invitation though I was very reluctant to leave the room.

Saturday, March 19

We went to the Gaieté Rochechouart, La Cigale, and La Lune Rousse.[18] The Inspector was right: It was good for me to get out and breathe the fresh air. At first, I had an uncomfortable feeling, as if I were doing something wrong; as if I were a deserter who had turned his back on the flag. But that soon went away. We

---

[18] All located in the Montmartre district of Paris, near *Place Pigalle*: *La Gaieté Rochechouart* was a famous Parisian café-music hall, popular in the late 19th century; opened in 1887, *La Cigale* (The Cicada) is a theater located at 120 *boulevard de Rochechouart*; and in the early 20th century, the *Cabaret de la Lune Rousse* (The Red Moon Cabaret) was a famous cabaret.

ends p. 26

drank a lot, laughed, and chatted. This morning, when I went to my window, Clarimonda gave me what I thought was a look of reproach, though I may only have imagined it. How could she have known that I had gone out last night? In any case, the look lasted only for an instant, then she smiled again.

We played the game all day long.

Sunday, March 20

Only one thing to record: we played the game.

Monday, March 21

We played the game—all day long.

Tuesday, March 22

Yes, the game. We played it again. And nothing else. Nothing at all.

Sometimes I wonder what is happening to me? What is it I want? Where is all this leading? I know the answer: there is nothing else I want except what is happening. It is what I want . . . what I long for. This only.

Clarimonda and I have spoken with each other in the course of the last few days, but very briefly; scarcely a word. Sometimes we moved our lips, but more often we just looked at each other with deep understanding.

I was right about Clarimonda's reproachful look because I went out with the Inspector last Friday. I asked her to forgive me. I said it was stupid of me, and spiteful to have gone. She forgave me, and I promised never to leave the window again. We kissed, pressing our lips against each of our windowpanes.

Wednesday, March 23

I know now that I love Clarimonda. That she has entered into the very fiber of my being. It may be that the loves of other men are different. But does there exist one head, one ear, one hand that is exactly like hundreds of millions of others? There are always differences, and it must be so with love. My love is strange, I know that, but is it any the less lovely because of that? Besides, my love makes me happy.

If only I were not so frightened. Sometimes my terror slumbers and I forget it for a few moments, then it wakes and does not leave me. The fear is like a poor mouse trying to escape the grip of a powerful serpent. Just wait a bit, poor sad terror. Very soon, the serpent love will devour you.

Thursday, March 24

I have made a discovery: I don't play with Clarimonda. She plays with me.

Last night, thinking as always about our game, I wrote down five new and intricate gesture patterns with which I intended to surprise Clarimonda today. I gave each gesture a number. Then I practiced the series, so I could do the motions as quickly as possible, forward or backward. Or sometimes only the even-numbered ones, sometimes the odd. Or the first and the last of the five patterns. It was tiring work, but it made me happy and seemed to bring Clarimonda closer to me. I practiced for hours until I got all the motions down pat, like clockwork.

This morning, I went to the window. Clarimonda and I greeted each other, then our game began. Back and forth! It

ends p. 26

was incredible how quickly she understood what was to be done; how she kept pace with me.

There was a knock at the door. It was the servant bringing me my shoes. I took them. On my way back to the window, my eye chanced to fall on the slip of paper on which I had noted my gesture patterns. It was then that I understood: in the game just finished, *I had not made use of a single one of my patterns.*

I reeled back and had to hold on to the chair to keep from falling. It was unbelievable. I read the paper again—and again. It was still true: I had gone through a long series of gestures at the window, and not one of the patterns had been mine.

I had the feeling, once more, that I was standing before Clarimonda's wide open door, through which, though I stared. I could see nothing but a dark void. I knew, too, that if I chose to turn from that door now. I might be saved; and that I still had the power to leave. And yet, I did not leave—because I felt myself at the very edge of the mystery: as if I were holding the secret in my hands. "Paris! You will conquer Paris," I thought. And in that instant, Paris was more powerful than Clarimonda.

I don't think about that any more. Now, I feel only love. Love, and a delicious terror.

Still, the moment itself endowed me with strength. I read my notes again, engraving the gestures on my mind. Then I went back to the window only to become aware that *there was not one of my patterns that I wanted to use.* Standing there, it occurred to me to rub the side of my nose; instead I found myself pressing my lips to the windowpane. I tried to drum with my fingers on the window sill; instead, I brushed my fingers through my hair. And so I understood that it was not that Clarimonda did what I did. Rather, my gestures followed her lead and with such lightning rapidity that we seemed to be moving simultaneously. I, who had been so proud because I thought I had been influencing her, I was in fact being influenced by her. Her influence . . . so gentle . . . so delightful.

I have tried another experiment. I clenched my hands and put them in my pockets firmly intending not to move them one bit. Clarimonda raised her hand and, smiling at me, made a scolding gesture with her finger. I did not budge, and yet I could feel how my right hand *wished* to leave my pocket. I shoved my fingers against the lining, but against my will, my hand left the pocket; my arm rose into the air. In my turn, I made a scolding gesture with my finger and smiled. It seemed to me that it was not I who was doing all this. It was a stranger whom I was watching. But, of course, I was mistaken. It was I making the gesture, and the person watching me was the stranger; that very same stranger who, not long ago, was so sure that he was on the edge of a great discovery. In any case, it was not I.

Of what use to me is this discovery? I am here to do Clarimonda's will. Clarimonda, whom I love with an anguished heart.

Friday, March 25

I have cut the telephone cord. I have no wish to be continually disturbed by the idiotic inspector just as the mysterious hour arrives.

God. Why did I write that? Not a word of it is true. It is as if someone else were directing my pen.

But I want to . . . want to . . . to write the truth here . . . though it is costing me great effort. But I want to . . . once more . . . do what I want.

I have cut the telephone cord . . . ah . . .

Because I had to . . . there it is. Had to . . .

We stood at our windows this morning and played the game, which is now different from what it was yesterday. Clarimonda makes a movement and I resist it for as long as I can. Then I

ends p. 26

give in and do what she wants without further struggle. I can hardly express what a joy it is to be so conquered; to surrender entirely to her will.

We played. All at once, she stood up and walked back into her room, where I could not see her; she was so engulfed by the dark. Then she came back with a desk telephone, like mine, in her hands. She smiled and set the telephone on the window sill, after which she took a knife and cut the cord. Then I carried my telephone to the window where I cut the cord. After that, I returned my phone to its place.

That's how it happened . . .

I sit at my desk where I have been drinking tea the servant brought me. He has come for the empty teapot, and I ask him for the time, since my watch isn't running properly. He says it is five fifteen. Five fifteen . . .

I know that if I look out of my window, Clarimonda will be there making a gesture that I will have to imitate. I will look just the same. Clarimonda is there, smiling. If only I could turn my eyes away from hers.

Now she parts the curtain. She takes the cord. It is red, just like the cord in my window. She ties a noose and hangs the cord on the hook in the window crossbar.

She sits down and smiles.

No. Fear is no longer what I feel. Rather, it is a sort of oppressive terror which I would not want to avoid for anything in the world. Its grip is irresistible, profoundly cruel, and voluptuous in its attraction.

I could go to the window, and do what she wants me to do, but I wait. I struggle. I resist though I feel a mounting fascination that becomes more intense each minute.

Here I am once more. Rashly, I went to the window where I did what Clarimonda wanted. I took the cord, tied a noose, and hung it on the hook . . .

Now, I want to see nothing else—except to stare at this paper. Because if I look. I know what she will do . . . now . . . at the sixth hour of the last day of the week. If I see her, I will have to do what she wants. Have to . . .

I won't see her . . .

I laugh. Loudly. No. I'm not laughing. Something is laughing in me, and I know why. It is because of my "I won't" . . .

I won't, and yet I know very well that I have to . . . have to look at her. I must . . . must . . . and then . . . all that follows.

If I still wait, it is only to prolong this exquisite torture. Yes, that's it. This breathless anguish is my supreme delight. I write quickly, quickly . . . just so I can continue to sit here; so I can attenuate these seconds of pain.

Again, terror. Again. I know that I will look toward her. That I will stand up. That I will hang myself.

That doesn't frighten me. That is beautiful . . . even precious.

There is something else. What will happen afterward? I don't know, but since my torment is so delicious. I feel . . . feel that something horrible must follow.

Think . . . think . . . Write something. Anything at all . . . to keep from looking toward her . . . My name . . . Richard Bracquemont. Richard Bracquemont . . . Richard Bracquemont . . . Richard . . .

I can't . . . go on. I must . . . no . . . no . . . must look at her . . . Richard Bracquemont . . . no . . . no more . . . Richard . . . Richard Bracque . . .

ends next p.

The inspector of the ninth precinct, after repeated and vain efforts to telephone Richard, arrived at the Hotel Stevens at 6:05. He found the body of the student Richard Bracquemont hanging from the crossbar of the window in room #7, in the same position as each of his three predecessors.

The expression on the student's face, however, was different, reflecting an appalling fear. Bracquemont's eyes were wide open and bulging from their sockets. His lips were drawn into a rictus,[19] and his jaws were clamped together. A huge black spider whose body was dotted with purple spots lay crushed and nearly bitten in two between his teeth.

On the table, there lay the student's journal. The inspector read it and went immediately to investigate the house across the street. What he learned was that the second floor of that building had not been lived in for many months.

---

[19] A mouth fixed in a grimace or expression of pain.

HONORARY HEATHEN

ClARimondA
is there,
Smiling.
If only
I could turn
MY EYES
AwAy from
herS.

www.ingramcontent.com/pod-product-compliance
Lightning Source LLC
Chambersburg PA
CBHW031000310726
48969CB00008B/2415